You're a Winner
Tractor Mac

Written and Illustrated by Billy Steers

For my sons,
Trip, Wil & Nate
Blue Ribbon Winners each!

The big event was almost here!
For months Tractor Mac and Farmer Bill had been getting ready
for the big tractor pull contest at the county fair.

"I can remember all the great horse pulls at the fair," said Sibley the workhorse.

"I'm sure I can pull the weights the farthest and win that contest!" said Mac. He felt as strong as ten tractors.

"I hope you win, Mac!" Said Tucker Pickup.

"WOOF YIP!" barked Fetch the dog.

Finally the day of the big pull came!
"Good luck!" bellowed Margot the cow as Tucker
pulled Mac to the fair.

The fairgrounds were full of things to see and do.
There were rides and a brightly painted carousel.
Music played and children laughed.
"This will be a happy day!" thought Tractor Mac.

The pulling arena was crowded with many tractors from all over.
Big blue ones. Huge orange ones. Giant green ones.

Tractor Mac suddenly felt very small.

The announcer called the tractors
to the ring one at a time.

Mac did great in his first round. He pulled the heavy blocks easily.
The Line Judge shouted, "FULL PULL!" when Tractor Mac had
reached the end of the track.

"The day's not over yet," said a big tractor named Deke.

"Only the *really* strong tractors make it to the finals."

The tractors had to work harder as the loads got heavier.
By midday, more than half of the tractors were out of the event.
They couldn't pull the weights far enough.

By late afternoon, only two tractors were left.
Tractor Mac and Deke.

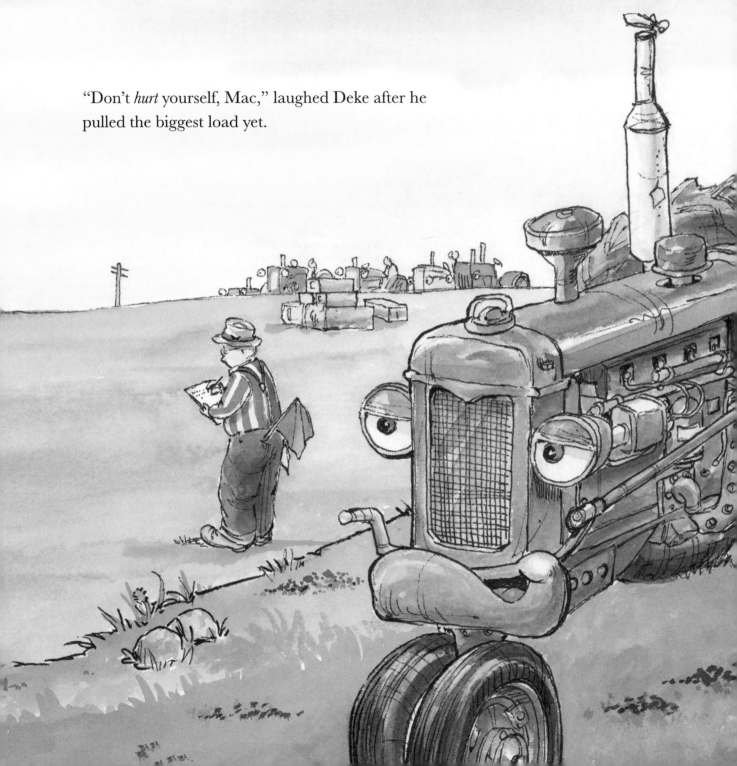

"Don't *hurt* yourself, Mac," laughed Deke after he pulled the biggest load yet.

It was Mac's turn again.
This was it!
"Do your best!" said a little bulldozer nearby.

Heave! *Tug!* **PULL**!

Mac pulled as hard as he could. The load inched forward, Mac's engine roared, and his tires bit into the sand. Finally he could pull no farther. The crowd waited to hear the judge's call.

Mac had been beaten!
Deke had pulled the same weight, but pulled it one foot farther.
Mac felt like crying as he watched Deke collect first prize.

Slowly, Tractor Mac left the arena
and passed through the fairground on his way out.
The carousel stood still and quiet. Fair workers were trying
to fix the broken generator. Children sadly watched and waited.
What an unhappy day this was.

Suddenly, Farmer Bill had an idea! He parked close
and hooked Mac's power belt to the carousel.

Mac throttled up, the belt spun, music played!
The colorful animals came to life, and laughing children
climbed back on board!
"Hooray for the big red tractor!" everyone shouted.

For the rest of the day, Mac helped run the carousel.
When it was time to go back home, he could hardly wait
to tell everything to his friends at the farm.
Farmer Bill smiled proudly and said,
"Tractor Mac, you're a *true* winner!"